VOLUME 1: BLACK CLOUD™ NO EXIT

Story	JASON LATOUR AND IVAN BRANDON
Script	IVAN BRANDON
Art	GREG HINKLE
Color	MATT WILSON
Color flats	DEE CUNNIFFE
Lettering	ADITYA BIDIKAR
Logo and design	TOM MULLER
Cover	GREG HINKLE AND MATT WILSON
Collection Editor	RACHEL PINNELAS
Original series editors	MARIA C. LUDWIG RACHEL PINNELAS

Chapter 1

BL
CLO

THE FUTURE WILL ALWAYS BE DARK.

FORMLESS.

EMPTY.

A BLANK PAGE WE FILL
WITH ASPIRATION.

AND WITH
DREAD.
BEWARE,
CHILDREN.
BAH.
STORIES WE TELL
OURSELVES.

FUTURE'S A MAGIC TRICK. A SLEIGHT OF HAND.
A **STORY.**

OUR STORIES SHAPED OUR WORLD.
AND BURNT IT.

CONJURED OUR RECKONING.

AND GAVE US HEROES.

WE TELL THESE STORIES TO OURSELVES, **STILL.** TO KEEP ON GOING.
LIKE DAYTIME SOAPS. STARRING THAT BOY WHO JUMPED THE TURNSTILE.
EPIC BATTLES AGAINST CUSTOMER SERVICE.
THEY LIFT US UP OR PIN US DOWN. PUT US ON THE STRAIGHT AND NARROW.
YOU, SIR. I SEE BIG THINGS FOR YOU.
A GIRL CAN DREAM
C'MON FOLKS, WHAT'S IT WORTH TO YOU?

TIPS
I DON'T ASK FOR ONE HUNDRED. JUST **ONE!**

YEAH, THE SAME WOMAN. OH, **NO,** HOLD ON...
TINK TINK

STORY'S THE ONLY THING THAT EVER MATTERED.

OR OFF A LEDGE.
GET A JOB, LADY.
CLINK
..NK
THEY CAN MAKE US BELIEVE IN THE IMPOSSIBLE.
OR JUST TELL US WHAT WE WANT TO HEAR.
ONE DOLLAR. IT'S ONLY ONE! EVERY DAY WITH THIS!
AND MY STORY?
WHY DO YOU DO THIS, LADY? WHY DO YOU DO THIS EVERY DAY TO ME?
...MY STORY SUCKS.
TIPS

WHAT IF I TOLD YOU I'M FROM A PLACE THAT SAW THIS ALL COMING?
THIS POINT IN TIME. ALL OF YOUR BRAINS SAUCED UP IN VIRAL CONTENT AND FANTASY SPORTS. BROADCAST REALITY.

I'M FROM A PLACE OF STORIES. SO BIG THEY DEFINED EVERYTHING.

PEOPLE SO COMMITTED TO THEIR STORIES THEY CHOSE TO LIVE IN THEM.
JUST OPENED A DOOR INTO ANOTHER FUTURE. AWAY FROM HERE.
WALKED THROUGH THAT DOOR AND NEVER BACK.

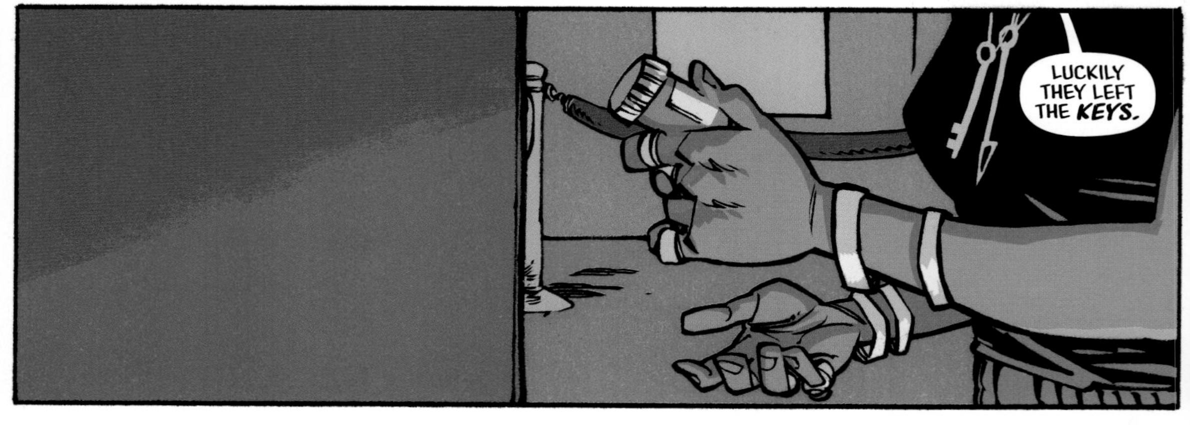
LUCKILY THEY LEFT THE KEYS.

WHY'S MINE LOOK LIKE A DINOSAUR?
WILL THIS INTERACT WITH MY ATIVAN?
YEAH...I MAYBE **DON'T** JUST PUT RANDOM PILLS IN MY MOUTH?

I GET SCARED MYSELF, I KNOW THE FEELING.

BUT YOU KNOW WHAT MIGHT BE PAST THAT **FEAR?** ELATION. **DELIGHT.**

YOU JUST GOTTA **BELIEVE** IN ME, THAT I WON'T LET YOU FALL.

TODD!

WHERE DID EVERYBODY ***GO?!***
WAIT, WHERE... WHERE ***AM*** I? OH GOD.
IS THIS NEW JERSEY?

WHAT DID SHE ***DO*** TO ME?
DOSED ME WITH SOME-THING.

SLOW DOWN, JACK. HAVE A DRINK.
I DON'T ***WANT*** A DRINK, MAN. I COULD BE ***POISONED!***

IS THERE A ***PROBLEM*** HERE?

WE DON'T LIKE TROUBLE HERE. YOU BRINGING TROUBLE?
NNNAAHH!!

OH GOD OH NO OH GOD...

WATCH IT, BOSS! SOME OF US ARE TRYING TO GET THROUGH THE NIGHT.

I'M FREAKING OUT, OH GOD SAVE ME.
SAVE ME, I SWEAR TO NANCY DAVIS REAGAN I WON'T EVER LOOK AT DRUGS AGAIN...

I GOT YOU, WALL STREET.

WAKING UP IN SOMEONE ELSE'S WORLD IS HARDER THAN YOU THINK.

EVEN MINE.
AM I SEEING THINGS?
I SEE HER TOO.

AT EASE, PEOPLE.

TODD. SWEETHEART. THIS ISN'T YOU.

TODD IS A BIG BOY. KNOWS WHAT HE WANTS.

AND HE KNOWS HOW TO GET IT.
HOW ARE YOU...HOW IS THIS... HAPPENING?
CALL IT A FAMILY SECRET.
I WON'T SAY YOUR NAME BECAUSE ONE OF US STILL RESPECTS THE RULES.

PLEASE TRUST THAT WE'RE AWASH IN OURSELVES JUST TO KNOW YOU STILL **REMEMBER** US.

BUT WE CAN **NOT** AFFORD YOUR TROUBLE HERE.

THE MAN SAID YOU'RE **DONE.** AND THIS IS **HIS** PLACE.
I HAVEN'T FINISHED MY DRINK.

YOU **SURE** IT'S HIS? I THINK I'VE MADE SOME **FRIENDS.**

YOU CAN KEEP MY NAME OFF YOUR LIPS, BUT I THINK THEY KNOW WHO I AM. THEY STILL REMEMBER MY STORY.

OH, I REMEMBER.

BUT I DON'T BUY IT ANYMORE.
THAT HAND DOESN'T GO.
AAGH!

ARE YOU CRAZY?
HEH.

DIDN'T YOU JUST PRAY TO NANCY REAGAN?

BELIEVE ME, TODD...

THE ONLY TROUBLE HERE...

IS ME.

-HUFF- THAT--THAT WAS -HUFF- TERRIFYING... THAT...THAT WAS...
GREAT... YOU WERE SO GREAT...
YOU SEE WHAT I CAN DO FOR YOU?
THIS IS JUST THE START.
I...
YOU CAN LIVE OUT A FAIRY TALE, TODD.
YOU CAN HAVE YOUR DREAMS. ONE BY ONE. UNTIL YOU'RE ALL OUT AND THEN I'LL FIND YOU BETTER DREAMS.
BECAUSE I BELIEVE IN YOU.
DO YOU BELIEVE IN ME?
YES.
OH NO.

WE HAVE TO GO.
WE WHAT? BUT WE JUST...
IT'S JUST A LITTLE RAIN.

NO...
IT'S NOT.
KRAKOOM
EVERY FAIRY TALE HAS MONSTERS.

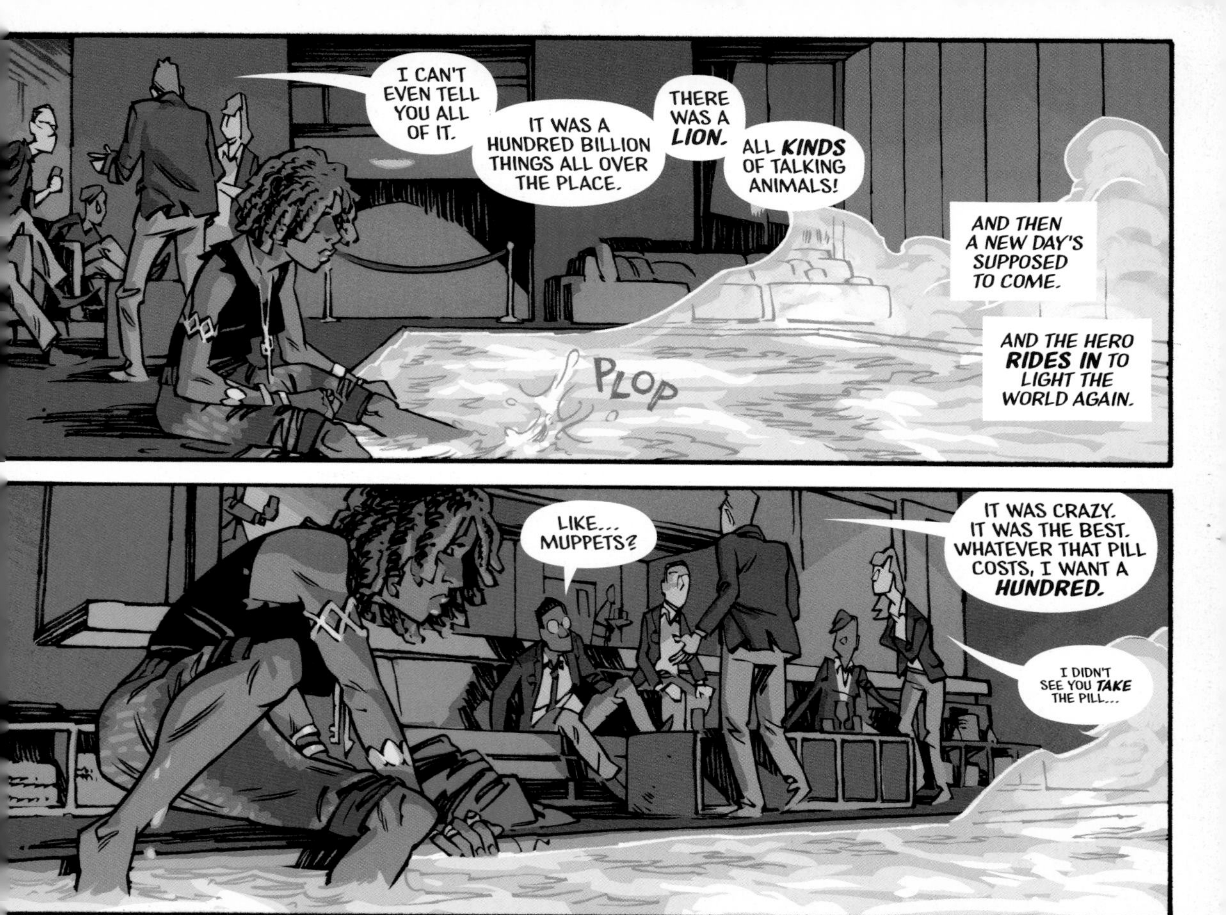
I CAN'T EVEN TELL YOU ALL OF IT.
IT WAS A HUNDRED BILLION THINGS ALL OVER THE PLACE.
THERE WAS A LION.
ALL KINDS OF TALKING ANIMALS!
AND THEN A NEW DAY'S SUPPOSED TO COME.
AND THE HERO RIDES IN TO LIGHT THE WORLD AGAIN.
PLOP
LIKE... MUPPETS?
IT WAS CRAZY. IT WAS THE BEST. WHATEVER THAT PILL COSTS, I WANT A HUNDRED.
I DIDN'T SEE YOU TAKE THE PILL...

I'M PRETTY SURE I'M NOT THE HERO OF MY STORY.

19 New Messages
I want more!!
I'm in!
BRING BACK MY PHONE YOU CRAZY LADY!!
Let me know where

WHERE I'M FROM, IT'S EASY TO LEAVE. BECAUSE NO ONE EVER **WANTS** TO.
BUT GOING THERE **COSTS.**

AND GETTING BACK...THE ENTRANCE CHANGES EVERY TIME. IT'S HARD TO FIND.
TAKING TODD TO THAT BAR WAS A BIG STUPID RISK.

BUT I HAD TO MAKE AN IMPRESSION.
I NEED DUMB KIDS WITH POCKETS I CAN EMPTY.
THE ONLY WAY I KNOW HOW TO **SURVIVE** UP HERE.

UP HERE WE HAVE NO PAST, NO PROSPECTS. NO ONE CARES ABOUT OUR STORIES. NO ONE **LISTENS.**
THOSE WHO MAKE IT OUT ARE MOSTLY ON THE STREET. BROKEN.

NO ONE WANTS TO TELL THAT STORY.

ALL MORNING THE PHONE HASN'T STOPPED JIGGLING.
RICH KID TEXTS, LIKE TINY STUPID POEMS.
"HEY, DID THAT REALLY HAPPEN?"
"RU A COP? U HAVE 2 TELL ME, RITE?"
"NEW PHONE, WHO DIS?"

AND THEN WEIRDEST OF ALL:
"THERE'S A CAR ON THE WAY. THE MAYOR WANTS TO MEET YOU."
DREAM HUGE Reelect DENNY HAVEMEYER
DREAM HUGE

YOU PUT ON QUITE A SHOW, I HEARD.
A DISAPPEARING ACT. KAY WAS VERY IMPRESSED.
I DON'T ASK WHY THERE'S A TEENAGER IN HIS EAR. THEN, LIKE HE'S IN MY HEAD...
KAY IS... A FRIEND.
A FRIEND.

WHAT SHE SAID WAS INTRIGUING. THE EXPERIENCE SEEMED UNLIKE ANYTHING I'VE HEARD, AND AS YOU CAN PROBABLY FIGURE, I HEAR A LOT.
ARE YOU OKAY? YOU SEEM...

CONFUSED, SIR.
DREAM HUGE
WHY DO YOU THINK YOU'RE HERE? DON'T WORRY, YOU CAN SPEAK FREELY.
HUGE

YOU GOT A MIC IN THAT TIE? OR THE CHIEF OF POLICE BEHIND DOOR NUMBER ONE?
MAYBE I'M HERE TO FIND OUT I CAN DISAPPEAR.

MS. BARRETT, I CAN HOPEFULLY ASSURE YOU THAT MY OFFICE ISN'T USED FOR ELABORATE STING OPERATIONS.
WELL, SIR, MISTER MAYOR, YOU DON'T STRIKE ME AS A GUY WITH A HABIT.

I HAVE NO TIME FOR ROUTINE, BUT I FIND MY MOMENTS. WE ALL HAVE NEED OF RECREATION.
IT IS PERHAPS THE ONLY WAY MY SON AND I ARE SIMILAR.
YOUR SON?
YOU MET HIM YESTERDAY. TODD. MY RECREATION IS MORE SUBTLE, PRIVATE. I DO WELL TELLING STORIES.
TODD...NEVER LEARNED THE VALUE OF WINNING HEARTS AND MINDS.

SO YOU WANT A TRIP?
I'D LIKE A DEMONSTRATION.
SIR, I CAN'T ALLOW YOU TO...
YOU DON'T ALLOW ME ANYTHING.

THOSE ARE SOME GREAT SPECS, YOUR HONOR. MAY I?

HUHH

SOME GUYS KNOW
WHAT TO WANT.

AND SOME GUYS
THINK THEY KNOW.

AND IF I THREAD THAT
NEEDLE I CAN EAT.

SIR, I CAN'T HEAR
YOU IF YOU'RE
WHISPERING...
SIGH
I SAID...
ANYTHING SHE
WANTS.
WAFFLES.
ALL OF THE
WAFFLES.

THE WORLD ABOVE, THIS WORLD IS TERRIFYING. WITHOUT THE STORY, IT'S JUST CHAOS.
MAPLE

LIKE ONE OF THOSE RICKETY RIDES GONE OFF THE RAILS AND AT A CLIFF.
I'M TRYING TO HOLD ON LIKE I HAVE A CHANCE, BUT I'M JUST WAITING ON IT ALL TO GO DARK.

BUT EVEN THROUGH MY GRITTED TEETH, SOMETIMES I HAVE TO LAUGH.
BZZZ
BZZ

BZZ
BZZZ
THE MAYOR THINKS HIS KID'S AN ASSHOLE, TOO.

AND HE'S HIRED ME TO MAKE HIM DISAPPEAR.

NOT FOREVER, HE ASSURES ME. JUST TILL HE'S RE-ELECTED.

ALL EXPENSES PAID. INFINITE OVERTIME.
THIS PLACE IS...
...UNBELIEVEABLE.

OH MY GOD, IT'S THAT BAR!
THE BEST BAR!

NOT TONIGHT.
DON'T BOIL OVER ALL AT ONCE, TODD, WE'RE ON A LONG VACATION.
THERE ARE OTHER BARS. AND EVERYTHING'S COVERED.

I SAID YOU'RE BANNED! YOU'RE EIGHTY-SIXED!
I DON'T CARE WHO THE FUCK YOU ARE.

YOU DON'T RUN ME OFF.

I CHOSE TO LEAVE.

YOU JERKS DON'T SEE STRAIGHT.

HRRRNGH...
I TOLDJA...
TOLDJA WE OUGHTA LET HER BE. SHE'S OLDBLOOD, MAN!
WHEN I LEFT I SAVED YOU ALL...

SAVED YOU FROM ME.
RRNNGG...
SKIP THIS.
NGGAAHH!
THOK

RAIN? AGAIN?
OH NO... NOT YET...

THAT'S RIGHT. I CALLED HIM.

HEY!
DON'T LEAVE ME!
DREAMS ARE EXPENSIVE.

EVEN HERE. EVEN FOR ME.

ALAS FOR TODD...

SLAM
I CAN'T AFFORD IT.

Chapter 2

DON'T YOU STEP AWAY FROM ME, DENNIS.
HONEY, I'VE GOT... WHAT HAVE I GOT AGAIN?
DREAM HUGE
HUGE
PRESS BRIEFING. ON THE BUDGET CHANGES.
I WANT TO KNOW WHERE HE IS, AND I WANT TO KNOW IT NOW.
WHERE IS MY SON?

HE'LL TURN UP, DOTTIE. HE ALWAYS TURNS UP.
YOU CAN LIE TO THE WHOLE CITY BUT YOU CAN'T LIE TO ME.
I KNOW WHAT IT SOUNDS LIKE.

MA'AM I'LL GET A DETAIL OUT THERE LOOKING. WE WILL FIND TODD AND BRING HIM BACK TO YOU. POLISHED UP LIKE NEW.
DREAM HUGE

GET THIS STUPID GOD-DAMNED--

--HAT OUT OF MY FACE.
YOU THINK I HAVEN'T SENT MY PEOPLE? I HAVEN'T LOOKED IN EVERY GODDAMNED PLACE THERE IS?

I KNOW YOU DID IT. I KNOW YOU SNUCK HIM OFF TO HIDE HIM FROM YOUR CAMPAIGN.
DOTTIE, YOU'RE GOING TO LISTEN, NOW.
NO. I'M GOING TO BE CLEAR. YOU GET HIM BACK TO ME.
OR YOU WON'T BE ABLE TO HIDE WHAT HAPPENS NEXT.

SIR, DON'T WORRY, WE...
GET AWAY FROM ME.

MADAM FIRST LADY.
NOT NOW.

NOW'S THE ONLY TIME WE HAVE. IT'S YOUR SON, TODD.
BUT IF THEY SEE ME, I WILL LOSE THIS JOB. AND I CAN'T LOSE THIS JOB.

IT'S NOT ON THE BOOKS, OR ANYWHERE IT CAN BE FOUND. BUT YESTERDAY HIS TEAM WAS SCRAMBLING.

WHAT DOES THAT MEAN?
RUNNING AROUND. MAKING ARRANGEMENTS, AT SOME REMOVE FROM OUR...OFFICIAL BUSINESS. CASH ARRANGEMENTS.

SPEAK IN ENGLISH. SAY WHAT YOU MEAN TO.
WE BOOKED A SUITE. OFF THE BOOKS. YOU UNDERSTAND ME NOW?

BL
CLO

THERE IS NO EASY WAY TO GET BACK FROM MY WORLD.
DON'T HAVE A TURNSTILE. NO MAGIC BRIDGE.
CLOSEST DESCRIPTION OF THE WAY IT WORKS...IS THAT YOU TRAVEL INSIDE-OUT.
BLACK FLAG, NOW.
RAISE YOU BACK UP.

AND WHEN YOU'RE THROUGH IT'S LIKE THE THING YOU WERE AND WHAT YOU ARE... ARE INCOMPATIBLE.
SHE DON'T NEED NO MORE.

BUT FIRST?
EXCUSE ME...DID YOU SEE HOW I... GOT HERE?

YOU DON'T REMEMBER ANYTHING.
DID...DID ANYBODY...?

THEN YOU JUST **WISH** YOU DIDN'T.
RAKOOM

Rain. Frank.

FRANK!!!

FRANK USED TO SAY, SEEING ME COMING...
"HERE COMES TROUBLE."
IT USED TO TWIST ME UP.
DID YOU HEAR HIM NOW? IT WAS A SIMPLE QUESTION.
ZELDA BARRETT.
I DON'T KNOW NO ZELDA! I NEVER MET ONE EVER! I SWEAR BY CHRIST AND MARY BOTH!
ALRIGHT, WE'LL TRY AGAIN.
WAIT...
TROUBLE'S TOO SMALL A WORD FOR ALL THE MESS I'VE MADE.
DREAM HUGE
MS. BARRETT.
WE'RE TASKED WITH DETERMINING THE RELATIVE HEALTH OF THE...SUBJECT IN YOUR...CARE.
...SUB...JECT?

TOM.
TODD!
SOMEBODY'S KID. (MAYOR?)

THEY THINK I HAVE HIM.
DO I HAVE HIM?
DON'T TOUCH ME.
I DON'T WORK FOR YOU. I DID NOT AGREE TO CARRY AGENTS ON MY BACK.

IF I LET THEM SEE ME SHAKE, I'M DONE.
YOU ALL BACK OFF OF ME.
I MADE A DEAL WITH SOMEONE HIGH ABOVE YOU AND THAT DEAL HAD A TERM.
AND WHEN THAT TERM IS UP, YOUR "SUBJECT" WILL APPEAR.

I SWEAR IF YOU DON'T MOVE I'LL SCREAM SO LOUD YOU'LL ALL BE ON THE NEWS IN FIFTEEN SECONDS.

WE HAD A DEAL. TELL HIM TO LEAVE YOUR STUPID FACES OUT OF MY WAY.
I HATE ME FOR LYING.
FOR RUNNING SCARED.

MOSTLY I HATE MYSELF FOR TRYING TO SNEAK BACK INTO MY OWN HOME.
BUT IF I DON'T GET THAT KID AND SHOW HIS FACE...

SHIT SHIT.

ALREADY SEEN YA.

NO YOU DIDN'T.

HAD TO BE LEM.
THAT FUCKING **GECKO** PUT YOU THERE?
WHO? ME?!
KINDA **LANGUAGE** IZZAT FOR KIDS?
NERP, NOT THE LIZARD.

hmph!
IT WAS **FRANK.**

HE WANTS TO **SEE** YOU, SAID.
SAID JUST TO TALK, IS ALL. EASY PEASY.
NOTHIN' TO BE SCARED ABOUT.
POOF!

WELL, I GOT A FULL PLATE, TELL HIM.
AND I'M **NOT** SCARED.
TELL YOUR HAND TO STOP SHAKIN', THEN.

NOT SCARED OF **FRANK.** I KNEW THAT GUY WHEN HE WAS **NOBODY.**
YEAH, I KNOW. NAME ME A SOME-BODY WHO WASN'T.

NOT SCARED AT ALL. ***I'M*** THE SCARY ONE.
GET IN THERE, GRAB THE KID AND GO. TEN SECONDS.
JUST NEED A WAY IN.
SMACK

SORRY. ***SORRY.***

I'M NOT SCARED.

OLD DAYS, I **RAN** THIS THING.

BREAK'S ONLY TEN **MINUTES,** FRANK.
COME ON. I'LL BE DONE WITH THIS IN **TWO,** TOPS.

SOMEHOW YOU'RE CUTE EVEN AT YOUR MOST **VILE.**
GUESS THAT'S **YOUR** STORY.

FANKSH. YOU SHOO.
LOOK AT THIS PLACE. WHAT A **DUMP.**

WHAT DO YOU **MEAN?** WHOLE DAY'S **SPECTACULAR.**
IT **SHOULDN'T** BE. TELL ME WHAT **YOU'RE** LOOKING AT. **DESCRIBE** IT, I MEAN. WHAT YOU **SEE.**

I SEE ALL THE SKIES MIXED UP LIKE SPICE. THIS WORLD AND THAT, BRAND NEW AND CRUMBLING. I SEE IDEAS.
ON TOP OF ALL OF THAT I SEE YOU, TWINKLING.

YEAH, THAT'S ALL **BULL**SHIT. THAT'S THE SAME THING **EVERYBODY** SEES.

STRONGEST IDEA WINS, **RIGHT?**
EXPLAIN **THAT** THEN. STACKED SO HIGH NOBODY'D EVER REACH THE TOP. AN **OVER**STATEMENT OF INTENT.
IT'S LITERALLY POKING THROUGH A CLOUD THAT NEVER MOVES.

NOPE
RULES ARE RULES, ZEL. AND THEY HAVE THEIR **PURPOSE.**

THE OLD-FATHERS...

RULES FOR **US,** DUMMY. TO PROTECT **THEM** FROM **US.**
SMACK

THEY SAY THEY BUILT ALL THIS SO THEY'D BE FREE, BUT THAT'S NOT THE TRUTH.
THEY LOST THEIR AUDIENCE.
SO NOW WE'RE IT. THIS WHOLE WORLD, STUCK IN THE FRONT ROW...
...WATCHING ALL THE THINGS THEY WANT US TO.

WHAT'S... HOW'D YOU...?

PICTURE A PLACE FAR OUT OF TOWN. HILLS THAT FEED INTO HILLS.

SO BIG IT BLOCKS THE SUN WHEREVER YOU GO. LIKE A **CROWN,** SNUG ON ITS HEAD.

OR YOU CAN SEE THE SAME OLD **BULLSHIT.**
IF YOU CAN... IF YOU CAN DO **THAT,** WHY ARE YOU STILL...
...WHY ARE YOU WORKING THIS STUPID DAYLIGHT SHIFT WITH **ME?**

BECAUSE I CAN'T DO IT BY **MYSELF.**

"BECAUSE I NEED HELP."

YOU GOT A QUESTION, LET ME KNOW.

I...UH.

THANK YOU. I'M GOOD.
YOU KNOW WE GOT CAMERAS, RIGHT? IN THE MODERN WORLD?

YOU DON'T STRIKE ME AS THE BEER TYPE, ZELDA.

I DIDN'T KNOW IT WAS... I DIDN'T...
COME ON, LET'S NOT START OFF THIS WAY. YOU WANT TO TALK, WE'LL GO IN BACK.

HAVEN'T SEEN YOU IN YEARS, ZEL. AND NEVER UP HERE IN THE WORLD.
YOU LOOK LIKE SHIT.
I JUST... I WANTED TO SAY I'M SORRY.
FOR WHAT I DID.

WHAT DID YOU DO, EXACTLY?
RALLIED SOME YOUNG AND DUMB AND SENT US CHARGING BLIND AT THE OLD GATES.
IT WAS A DUMB MOVE, BUT IT WAS MINE TO MAKE. I COULD'VE WALKED. I COULD HAVE TOLD SOMEONE.

BUT I BELIEVED YOU.
ALL OF YOUR CRAZY BULLSHIT, HOOK AND LINE. YOU TELL A STORY... MAYBE BETTER THAN ANYONE.

I MEANT... FRANK.
HEH HEH...OH GOD.
YOU THINK I'M MAD BECAUSE'A FRANK? LET'S BAR THE DOOR ON THAT CATFIGHT CLICHÉ, HUH?
THAT BOAT WAS SUNK A MONTH, AT LEAST. HE AND ME, WE BARELY SPOKE. AND NEVER REALLY.
WHAT BURNED ME UP WAS THAT I LISTENED. BUT DIDN'T THINK.
AND WHEN IT ALL WENT UPSIDE DOWN, THE OLDFATHERS SMOTHERING OUR LITTLE REVOLUTION...
...POOF, ZELDA WAS GONE.
YOU SEE ALL THIS? I MADE THE WHOLE THING OUT OF NOTHING, WITH MY HANDS. THIS IS ALL MINE.
YOU AND FRANK, YOU ALWAYS THOUGHT YOU WERE UNCOMPROMISED.
I THINK YOU'RE CHILDREN.

AND NOW OF COURSE YOU WANT SOME-THING.
AND YOU MUST BE UP A CREEK TO DRAG YOURSELF IN HERE IN FRONT OF ME.

HE LOCKED ME OUT, NAOMI.
WELL, GOOD FOR HIM.

WAAAAIT. YOU THINK I'M GONNA LET YOU BACK IN? OH, ZEL.

I DON'T BLAME YOU FOR WANTING TO TAKE THE SHORTCUT.
BUT DO YOU SEE A THEME, HERE? YOUR WHOLE LIFE'S A CHEATCODE.

"SO I CAN'T HELP YOU.
"BUT THESE DOORS AREN'T THE ONLY WAY IN, AND YOU KNOW IT."

"YOU KNOW THE OTHER WAYS. THE OLD WAYS.
"BUT YOU DON'T WANT TO.
"YOU THINK YOU DESERVE THIS PLACE.

"MAYBE THERE'S NOTHING TO LOSE, YOU EVER THINK OF THAT?"

"YOU EVER STOP TO THINK THAT MAYBE **BOTH** THESE WORLDS ARE BETTER OFF ***WITHOUT*** YOU?"

Chapter 3

IF YOU THINK YOU KNOW THE THINGS YOU ARE, THEN YOU'RE A LIAR.

YOUR PAST IS A STORY.
THE FUTURE'S BLANK.

ONCE YOU SETTLE ON ALL THAT?
YOU SEE YOU'RE WELL AND TRULY **FUCKED.**

BEWARE, CHILDREN.

MAYBE...
...FRANK MADE ME GO THIS WAY ON PURPOSE.
WITHOUT A DOOR, THE ONLY WAY IN IS TO GO BACK.
SIFT THROUGH IT ALL AGAIN TO FIND A HOLE.
A HOLE IN MY STORY.

WHERE DID IT COME FROM?

THE BEAST WAS MY CREATION, ZELDA.
OR MAYBE NOT.

EITHER WAY, THE PEOPLE NEEDED IT TO BE, AND SO I CALLED IT HERE.

WHAT COULD THE PEOPLE NEED A MONSTER FOR?

ISN'T IT OBVIOUS?
THEY NEEDED TO SEE THE BEAST SLAIN.

BL
CL

YOU THINK IT'S ALWAYS BEEN LIKE THIS?
EVEN THE OLD WORLD HAD MORE POTENTIAL THAN THIS DUMP.
WE LEFT THAT PLACE BEHIND FOR SOMETHING BETTER, THIS PLACE...
...WHERE "ANYTHING IS POSSIBLE".
IT'S WHAT THEY PROMISED.
OH NO, NOT AGAIN.
A MERITOCRACY. WHERE YOU COULD MOVE AHEAD BY BEING BETTER. THAT THOSE BEST IDEAS WOULD STAND TALLER THAN THE REST.
WHAT'D WE GET INSTEAD? ALL THIS. WE'RE AT EACH OTHER'S THROATS, GROWLING SO HARD THAT WE CAN'T HEAR THEM LOOKING DOWN, LAUGHING.
ME AGAINST YOU AND YOU AGAINST ME. AND WHY?
STOP. JUST STOP.
BECAUSE WE'RE PUPPETS.
WE'RE S'POSED TO BE MORE. AT LEAST ABOVE THEY KNOW HOW LAME EVERYTHING IS.

ABOVE. THE OLD WORLD.
YOU THINK IT'S DIFFERENT THERE THAN HERE? IF THEY'RE DECLINING, WE ARE BUSTED OUT.

THIS IS THE ROLE OF WHO'S NEXT. TO TEAR DOWN THE TACKY OLD WORLD AND WIPE THE DUST AWAY.

TO STEAL THE KEYS TO THE FUTURE WHILE THEY SLEEP.
AND IF THEY WAKE UP, KNOCK 'EM DOWN AGAIN.

YOU CAN SELL A LINE LIKE NO ONE ELSE. IT JUST SOUNDS RIGHT, DON'T IT?
BUT NO ONE CAN TAKE DOWN THE OLD BLOOD. OLD BLOOD'S THE WORLD ITSELF.

DON'T HAVE TO BEAT 'EM ALL. WE DON'T EVEN HAVE TO WIN.

JUST GOTTA SHOW THEM THEY CAN LOSE.
DON'T DO THIS. PLEASE.

"WHAT COULD THE PEOPLE NEED A MONSTER FOR?"

"ISN'T IT OBVIOUS?"

"THEY NEEDED TO SEE THE BEAST SLAIN."

YOU DID IT.

NOW EVERYTHING CHANGES.

YOUR MARK IS CLEAR.
YOU HAVE DISPROVED THE IMPOSSIBLE.
ABRADED BONDS THAT HAVE HELD THROUGH TO TIME BEFORE.

BUT NOW IT WILL STOP.

THE RIFT YOU MADE WILL GROW BEYOND WHAT YOU IMAGINED.

IT WILL SEEP AND FLOW BELOW YOUR FEET UNTIL THIS PLACE IS GONE.

THE ABSENCE MUST BE FILLED.
MY FAMILY'S SEAT. I WON.

BUT WINNING'S TOO GOOD FOR ME.
THE CLOUD CLAN SEAT IS OVERTURNED!
THE GARRISON NOW RISES!
WAIT! THERE. RIGHT THERE.
THE USURPER FLEES! WHAT SAY THE COUNCIL?!

EXILE.
EXILE.
EXILE.
EXILE.
EXILE.
EXILE.

EXILE.
THAT'S THE HOLE IN MY STORY.

YOUR PAST'S A STORY.

YOUR FUTURE'S PROBABLY A MESS.
THUD
RELAX. THAT'S NOT WHAT I'M HERE FOR.
YOU'VE BEEN GONE A LOT LONGER THAN YOU KNOW.
I NEVER LEARNED THAT TRICK. I CAN DO SHAPES, COLOR. BUT TIME...ONLY THE OLD ONES LIKE YOU CAN MIX UP TIME.
FUCK'RE YOU SLITHERING ABOUT?

MY HEAD'S COLLAPSING. TALK LIKE SOMEONE PEOPLE WANT TO LISTEN TO, LEM.
NO. YOU DON'T GET...AFTER WHAT YOU'VE DONE, AGAIN...
YOU DON'T GET TO TALK THAT WAY TO ME!
I WAS SLEEPING! ASLEEP! WHAT COULD I POSSIBLY HAVE DONE?!
WAR, YOU IDIOT.
YOUR STUPID WAR FINALLY SHOWED BACK UP.

BUT THIS TIME I'M NOT PLAYING. I DON'T CARE ABOUT YOUR SIDE OR ANYBODY ELSE'S.
I JUST WANTED THIS ONE THING, FOR ME. AND YOU HAD TO FILL THEIR STUPID HEADS WITH FIRE AND SMOKE.

I DON'T LIVE HERE ANYMORE! THERE'S NO ONE LEFT TO...

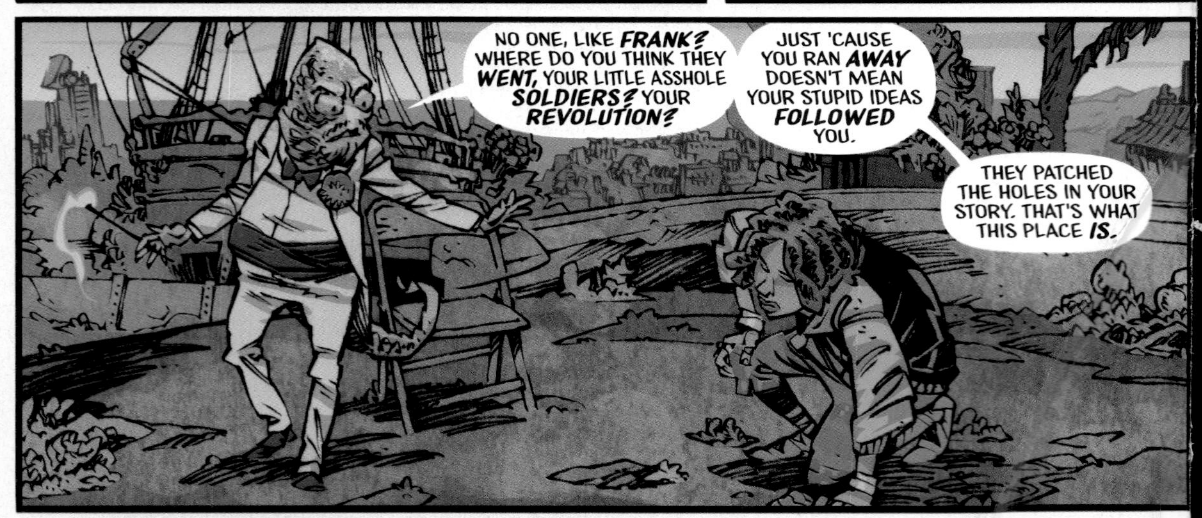
NO ONE, LIKE FRANK? WHERE DO YOU THINK THEY WENT, YOUR LITTLE ASSHOLE SOLDIERS? YOUR REVOLUTION?
JUST 'CAUSE YOU RAN AWAY DOESN'T MEAN YOUR STUPID IDEAS FOLLOWED YOU.
THEY PATCHED THE HOLES IN YOUR STORY. THAT'S WHAT THIS PLACE IS.

AND NOW HOW DO I HIDE?

HOW DO I HIDE FROM WHAT YOU'VE **DONE** TO US?
OH MY GOD.
...TODD?

"YOU LEFT HIM OUT IN THE RAIN."

FRANK...AT THE BAR, YOU DIDN'T CALL HIM 'CAUSE WE USED TO BE...

RIGHT, FRANK... FRANK IS IN CHARGE NOW.
Y'KNOW THAT FEELING, WHEN YOUR WHOLE WORLD TIPS ONTO ITS SIDE?

YOU WANNA FLOAT AWAY...

BUT YOU CAN'T MOVE UNDER THE CRUSHING WEIGHT OF KNOWING THIS IS ALL YOUR FAULT.
I NEED TO GET TO FRANK. CALL HIM AGAIN.
IT DOESN'T WORK LIKE THAT, GAVE ME A NUMBER THAT WON'T RING TWICE. TOLD ME TO USE IT WHEN YOU CAME BACK.
I'LL LIGHT A FIRE TO BRING HIM HERE. MADE OUT OF YOU.
I NEVER THOUGHT I'D MISS THAT SOUND.

HEY BOSS.
HI, ZEL. WELCOME HOME.
YOU'RE JUST IN TIME TO WATCH THE FIREWORKS.

Chapter 4

WE'RE ALL IMPRESSED YOU MADE IT BACK, CAPTAIN.

TAKES A HELL OF AN EGO TO COME APART AND THEN KNIT YOURSELF BACK TOGETHER ON THE OTHER SIDE.
YOU MUST BE TIRED, HUH.
WEAK.
DEAD TIRED.
OR MAYBE YOU'RE GETTING TOO MUCH CREDIT.
WHEN YOU'RE ONLY HERE BECAUSE FRANK WANTED YOU TO GET HERE.
I DON'T NEED PERMISSION TO GET THROUGH. I GREW UP HERE.
NO, YOU'RE A BIG GIRL, HUH? SO TELL ME THIS... IF YOU WEREN'T TRAPPED OUTSIDE THE DOOR...

"WHERE HAVE YOU BEEN?

"SHOW ME THE SUNSET YOU RODE INTO.

"WHAT A HAPPY ENDING YOU MUSTA FOUND, TO TAKE YOU AWAY FROM ALL OF WHAT WE'D WORKED FOR.
HELP
HELP
HELP WANTED

SOMEHOW YOU WEREN'T TOO BUSY TO LEAVE A FLAMING BAG OF SHIT ON OUR FRONT STEP.
SO WHERE'D YOU GO, BOSS? WHY ARE YOU STANDING HERE NOW?
YOU SHOULD BE RUNNING FOR YOUR LIFE.

YOU GIVE ADVICE THAT'S SOUND! MY BEST TO THOSE YOU LOVE!
STICK TO THAT WALL, LEM.

DON'T TURN YOUR FACE, I'VE SEEN YOU SCARED BEFORE.

I'M NOT SCARED.

POP
AT LEAST NOT FOR ME.

I WAS BORN TO RUN THIS PLACE. YOU KNOW HOW ALL ROADS LEAD TO ROME?
ZAP
WELL, ROME WAS ME.
THE BEST VERSION OF EVERY-THING THIS WORLD HAD HEADED FOR. A LIGHT SO BRIGHT I HAD TO BE THE FUTURE.

HELP ME UP...

TURNED OUT THE LIGHT WAS JUST A FIRE.
PLEASE DON'T. PLEASE STAY DOWN.

YOU DONE... ALREADY? YOU NEVER... DID...PUT IN THE WORK.
I DON'T WANT THIS.
ZAP
WE... BELIEVED IN YOU...CAN YOU IMAGINE?
AND THEN YOU LEFT US ALL TO DROWN.
ZZZZAAPP

THIS IS MY BETTER WORLD.
THIS IS THE DREAM I GOT THEM ALL TO BUY.

PLEASE, LEM.

DON'T MAKE ME HURT ANYONE ELSE.
WHERE IS HE?

DON'T!
YOU KNOW WHERE HE IS!

AND IF YOU SIT DON'T MAKE A SOUND...

WITH YOUR FEET OFF OF THE GROUND...

"HE'S WHERE YOU LEFT HIM."

...THAT GREY SOUND FROM A TIME SO STRANGE...

YOU GOT THE WORDS WRONG. BUT I GUESS THEY'D SUE YOU EVEN HERE.
I'D FORGOTTEN WHAT YOU LOOKED LIKE.

YOU'RE NOT SUPPOSED TO BE HERE ANYMORE.

WHERE ARE THE OLDFATHERS, FRANK?

YOU DON'T GET TO ASK ABOUT THIS PLACE.

YOU'VE BEEN GONE SO LONG IT'S LIKE YOU WEREN'T EVER HERE.
LOOKS LIKE YOU DID OKAY WITHOUT ME.
I WAS...

IF YOU SAY "WORRIED", YOU GO OUT THAT WINDOW.

IT WAS ALL A LIE, FRANK. I COULDN'T WASH IT DOWN. A MERITOCRACY OF IDEAS?
WE WERE JUST STUPID KIDS.

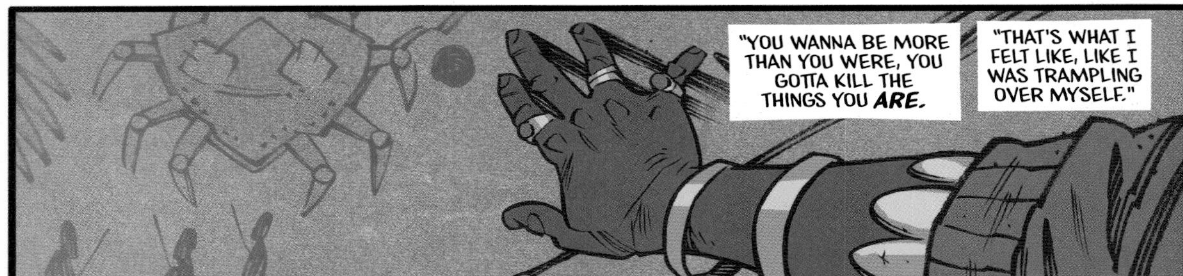
"YOU WANNA BE MORE THAN YOU WERE, YOU GOTTA KILL THE THINGS YOU ARE.
"THAT'S WHAT I FELT LIKE, LIKE I WAS TRAMPLING OVER MYSELF."

EACH OF THESE SEATS BOUND ALL THESE GEEZERS TO A LIE.
THAT THE WORLD LOOKS BETTER FROM ABOVE IT.
I DON'T HAVE A LOT NOW, BUT I'M FREE.

YOU SELL A LINE OF BULLSHIT LIKE A CHAMP.
SELL ME MY OWN HEAD ON A PLATE.

YOU CAN'T STOP HIDING, EVEN HERE. JUST TALKING TO THE FLOOR.

BUT YOU'RE GONNA *LOOK* AT ME.

THIS WHOLE *PLACE* IS SMOKING FROM A MATCH YOU THREW FOR *KICKS.*
I DON'T WANNA *HEAR* ABOUT HOW FREE YOU ARE TO ROLL THE *NEXT* PLACE.

"EVEN OUT *THERE* YOU'RE WORKING A CON.
"THAT GIANT MANBABY OUTSIDE...
"YOU THOUGHT YOU HAD HIS MAYOR DAD WRAPPED IN A *BOW.*

"YOU LET US CHOKE ON ALL THE DREAMS YOU SOLD US.
"YOU WANT A MERITOCRACY... AS LONG AS EVERYBODY KNOWS YOU'RE *BETTER.*

"THAT DEAD CAT OUTSIDE FINALLY HEARD THE *TRUTH,* THOUGH."

YOU ALWAYS HAD A WAY OF GETTING THROUGH MY NOISE.
YOU KNOW YOU'RE RIGHT.
BUT IF I'D HAVE STAYED HERE ALL THIS WOULD BE GONE. I CAN'T HAVE THIS POWER IN MY HANDS.
THIS IS YOU SAVING US?
I WANT TO FIX IT. I KNOW I'VE GOT NO RIGHT TO ASK FOR YOU TO HELP.

I GO BACK AND FORTH ON YOU, ZEL. LIKE-- CAN YOU HELP IT?

ARE YOU JUST THIS WIND THAT TEARS THROUGH EVERY-THING?
UNTIL IT CAN'T?

"BUT THERE'S NO CAN'T WITH YOU.

"YOU'RE PROBABLY THE END OF THE WORLD."

FRANK, I...

ZZZT
DO YOU KNOW WHAT HAPPENED WHEN YOU LEFT ME HERE? HOLDING THE BAG?

"DO YOU EVEN KNOW WHAT I HAD TO BE? JUST TO KEEP ON BREATHING.

"I WOULD'VE RUN WITH YOU, WHEREVER. I WOULD'VE LEFT ALL OF IT, LEFT ANYTHING.

INSTEAD OF THIS.
FRANK, WHERE ARE THE OLDFATHERS?

"WE FOUGHT YOUR WAR, ZEL.
"WE WON."

BUT NOTHING CHANGED. WE TOOK THE SYSTEM AND THE RULES AND WHEN IT WAS GONE ALL WE HAD LEFT WAS THE ANGER.

"IT'S NOT A WORLD OF FIGHTERS. THEY JUST BICKER. THEY RUN IN CIRCLES FOR THESE TINY PERSONAL VICTORIES TIL THEY'RE OUT OF BREATH.
"WE POINTED OUT ALL THE CRACKS IN THE STORY, BUT NO ONE KNEW HOW TO FIX THEM.

"THAT KID TODD, THEY TOOK TO HIM LIKE BUGS TO SHIT.
"YOU HAD TO KNOW THEY WOULD, HE'S LIKE ALL THE LIES THEY TELL THEMSELVES IN KHAKI FORM.
"HE DOESN'T CARE IT'S BROKEN. IT'S LIKE A BIG TOY TO HIM.
"HE JUST WANTS TO HAVE IT."
SNIFF
SNIFF

"YOU ALWAYS KNEW HOW TO TAKE THINGS APART, ZEL. YOU HAD THE EGO TO BREAK ANYTHING.

BUT YOU'D RUN OFF WHEN IT WAS TIME TO PUT THEM BACK TOGETHER. MAYBE YOU WERE SCARED.
OR MAYBE IT BORED YOU? LIKE YOU WERE FIVE, YOU'D GET ANNOYED AND SAY YOU FOUND IT THAT WAY.

"YOU WANT TO KNOW WHAT HAPPENED TO THE OLDFATHERS?

"THEY DIS-APPEARED. SAW WHAT WAS LEFT HERE AND WERE GONE.
"MAYBE THEY COULDN'T FIX IT.
"MAYBE THEY DIDN'T WANT TO BOTHER."

SO ALL THAT'S LEFT HERE NOW IS US.

US AND THIS MESS WE MADE.

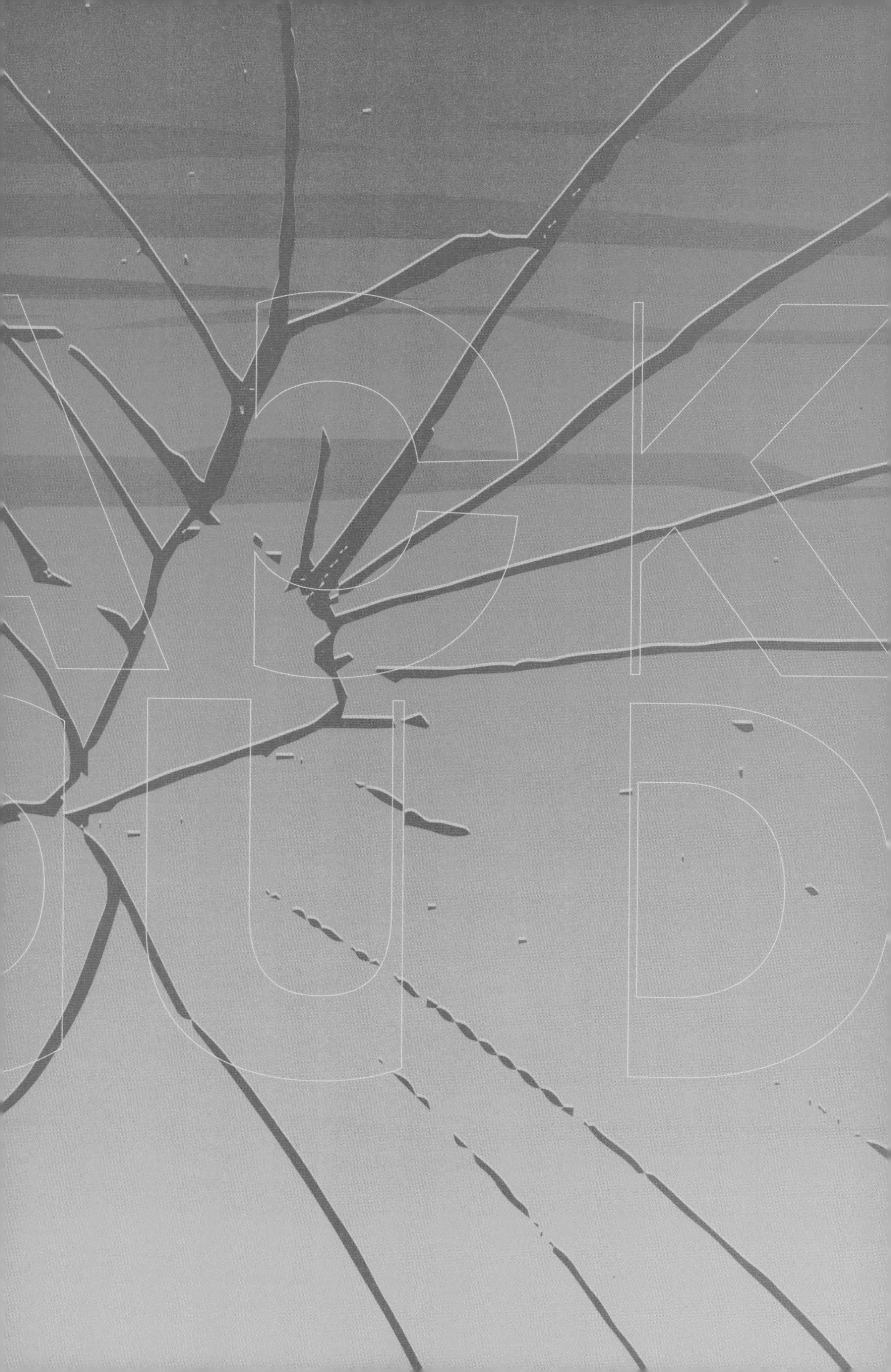

Chapter 5

LET'S SEE, WHERE WERE WE?

YEAH, WHERE WE ALWAYS ARE.
MAKING A MESS.

I'M GONNA HAVE TO FIX THAT TOO, NOW.

AFTER I FIGURE HOW TO GET HIS BIG ASS BACK HOME.
YOU GOT YOUR CART AND HORSE ALL MIXED.

WHOA.

THAT WAS AWESOME. I THINK I GOT A CHUB.

I NEVER DREAMED OF THINGS LIKE THIS. MAYBE I NEVER DREAMED OF ANYTHING.

LOOK AT 'EM! ALL FREAKING OUT...I NEVER FELT LIKE THIS BEFORE.

HE'S GROWING, WHY IS HE GROWING?
YOU KNOW WHY. FEAR IS A HELL OF AN OPIATE.

AT FIRST THEY WERE SCARED OF TODD BECAUSE THEY THOUGHT HE SPOKE FOR YOU.
BUT YOU'VE BEEN GONE SO LONG...
NOW THEY'RE JUST SCARED FROM BEING SCARED.
YOU HAVE ADVICE, OR YOU JUST ROLLING YOUR EYES FOR EXERCISE?

HEARTS AND MINDS, ZELDA.
YOU'RE NOT GONNA BEAT HIM WITH YOUR HANDS.

C'MERE YOU!

FRANK! SERIOUSLY?

WHY WOULD ANYBODY EVER LEAVE THIS PLACE?

OH, YOU HAVE NO IDEA.
HAVE YOU EVEN SEEN ALL THIS?

THOOM

I DON'T REMEMBER WHAT I HAD BEFORE I MET YOU.

ZELDA...?
PLEASE GOD, DON'T LET HER BE DEAD.

NO.
NOT DEAD.
I HAVEN'T FALLEN FAR ENOUGH YET.
HEY. BIGHEAD.

LET'S GET SERIOUS.
SHE CAN'T WIN, BOSS.
BOOM

DON'T NEED ME TELLING IT TO YOU.

YOU KNOW HER. THE REAL TRUTH OF WHO SHE IS.

EVEN IF SHE WON WE'D ALL OF US LOSE.

BL
CL

YOU JUST SIT STILL AND WE CAN GET YOU HOME.

HEY!
QUIT THAT!

YOU BROUGHT ME HERE.

SWAT
THIS IS MY HOME NOW.

CAN SOME-BODY TELL THIS DUDE THAT I'M SUPPOSED TO WIN?
I BET THE GERMANS HAVE A WORD.
FOR WHEN YOU'VE HURT SOMEONE SO BAD IT'S LIKE IT HURTS YOU JUST TO KNOW HOW THEY MUST FEEL.
OR JUST TO SEE THE BAD THAT YOU CAN DO.
BUT NOT ENOUGH TO STOP.
ALL THIS TIME I SAID I RAN AWAY FROM CONSEQUENCES.
FROM RETRIBUTION.
BUT IT WAS JUST THOSE EYES I COULDN'T FACE.

THIS IS MY STORY.
EVERY CHAPTER ENDS THE SAME.
THIS IS **CLASSIC** ME.

THESE PANTS ARE DRY-CLEAN ONLY!
I GET WHAT I WANT.

AND EVERYBODY GETS THE BILL.

HEY! AHOY! SLOW DOWN!

PISS OFF.
HEY! STOP!

RRRGGGH. I HATE THIS PLACE.
I GUESS IT'S MY TURN, FRANK. I SKIPPED OUT ON ALL THE OTHER ROUNDS.

IF HE DIES HERE I'M DEAD UP THERE, FRANK.
IF HE STAYS HERE WE'LL ALL BE GONE.
AND IF I STAY--
NOTHING CHANGES.
"THEY NEEDED TO SEE THE BEAST SLAIN."

STRING THE LAST IDEAS TOGETHER.
HOLD TIGHT, FRANK.
KLIK
THIS IS PROBABLY GONNA HURT ONE OF US.

WHUMP
THIS ARMOR SERVED MY MOM, HER DAD BEFORE, MY GRANDMA'S GRANDMA.
ALL DOWN THE LINE THE BEST IN SHOW. TOP OF OUR CLASS.
IT'S BIG ENOUGH TO FIT MY EGO. BUT ALL THAT, AND HISTORY, MAKE THIS ARMOR... HEAVY.

A WEIGHT I'VE CARRIED MY WHOLE LIFE.
LET IT SINK SOMEBODY ELSE FOR A CHANGE.
TOO DEEP.
NO OTHER WAY OUT...
...BUT TO LET GO.
I FEEL LIKE NOTHING, FLOATING UP.

I FEEL SO WEAK I ALMOST
DON'T KNOW WHO I **AM.**

CHRIST, STATEN ISLAND.
THIS I REMEMBER?

YOU SAID TO BELIEVE IN YOU AND I DID. BUT YOU'RE A BIG DUMB JERK.

DO YOUSE SEE THAT?

PLEASE, FRANK, JUST TRUST ME ONE LAST TIME.

THIS THING IS GROSS AND SO ARE YOU.
PLEASE, FRANK.

PLEASE?
HUK

THANK YOU.
C'MON, PUT YOUR BACKS IN, HELP THE NUTBAG OUT.
HIS HEAD'S TOO BIG TO BRING HIM BACK. TOO BIG TO FALL APART BETWEEN BOTH WORLDS.

BEST WE CAN DO IS PUT A PIN IN IT.
GET THE MESS STUCK IN THE MIDDLE. UNDER THE RUG UNTIL I KNOW HOW TO DEAL WITH HIM.

UNTIL I GET SOME...

THE MAYOR ASKS AGAIN FOR ANY NEWS AS TO THE WHEREABOUTS OF HIS SON TODD...
TODD HAVEMEYER, WHO HAS BEEN MISSING SINCE BEFORE THE ELECTION...
MAYOR MIGHT BE GREAT WITH HIS SON AWAY, BUT DOTTIE ISN'T.
BREAKING NEWS
WHAT KIND OF MONSTERS ARE THESE? TO TAKE A MOTHER'S ONLY BOY?
THE CITY WILL NOT REST UNTIL IT'S SAFE FOR MY SON AND THE COUNTLESS CHILDREN WHO GO MISSING EVERY YEAR.
...POLLSTERS SAY THE DISAPPEARANCE OF THE MAYOR'S SON HELPED HIM ACHIEVE A LANDSLIDE RE-ELECTION...
BACK HERE, YOU PUNK TRASH!

HA! WHERE YOU EVEN THINK YOU'RE RUNNING TO?
C'MON, JULIE! C'MON!
HNF HNF
THEY'RE USING THIS TO RATTLE CAGES. "CLEAN UP THE STREETS." EVEN UP HERE I CAN SCREW IT UP FOR EVERYONE.

I JUST WANNA CRAWL ON INTO NOTHING. STOP TRACKING MUD OVER THE WORLD.
PLEASE, STOP! WE'RE JUST KIDS, MISTER!

THAT'S HOW WE GOT INTO THIS MESS.
UNNGNNF!

GO! GET *OUTTA* HERE!

YOU TOO, LADY, THESE GUYS'LL MAKE YOU INTO HAM-BURGERS.

YEAH, GET *RUNNING*. THAT'S ALL YOUR KIND HAS LEFT TO DO. *WE* RUN THIS NOW.
DREAM HUGE

YOU GO ON, KID.
RUN FOR IT.

I'LL CATCH UP.

Cover Gallery

BLACK CLOUD #1

BLACK CLOUD #1
C2E2 exclusive cover

JASON LATOUR IVAN BRANDON GREG HINKLE MATT WILSON
1

BLACK CLOUD™

BLACK CLOUD #1
Fried Pie Con variant

JASON LATOUR IVAN BRANDON GREG HINKLE MATT WILSON
2
$ 3.99

BLACK CLOUD™

BLACK CLOUD #2

BLACK CLOUD #2
Spawn anniversary variant

JASON LATOUR IVAN BRANDON GREG HINKLE MATT WILSON
3
$ 3.99
BLACK CLOUD

BLACK CLOUD #3

JASON LATOUR IVAN BRANDON GREG HINKLE MATT WILSON
4
$ 3.99

BLACK CLOUD™

BLACK CLOUD #4

BLACK CLOUD #5

imagecomics.com